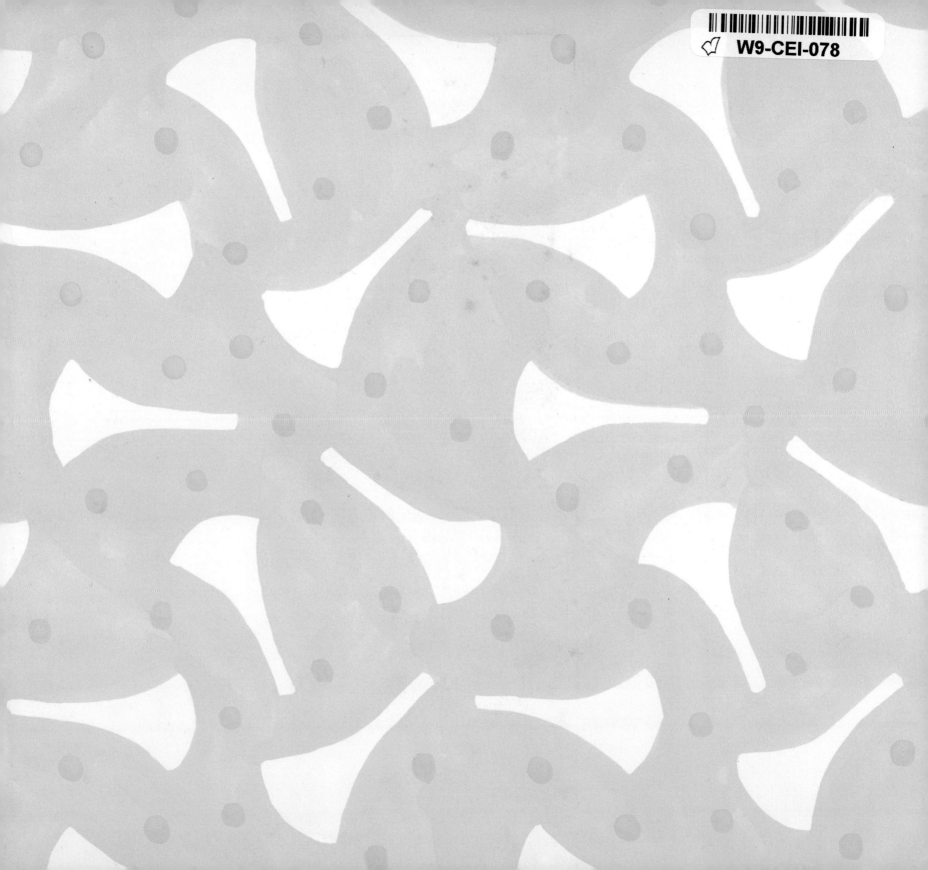

For Tom

Library of Congress Cataloging-in-Publication Data

Imai, Miko, 1963–
Sebastian's trumpet / Miko Imai. — 1st ed.
Summary: When he and his brothers get instruments for their birthday,
Sebastian is frustrated because he cannot play his trumpet right away.
ISBN 1-56402-359-1
[1. Trumpet—Fiction. 2. Musical instruments—Fiction.
3. Brothers—Fiction.] I. Title.
PZ7. I333Se 1995
[E]—dc20   94-47191

2 4 6 8 10 9 7 5 3 1

Printed in Hong Kong

The pictures in this book were done in gouache.

Candlewick Press
2067 Massachusetts Avenue
Cambridge, Massachusetts 02140

SEBASTIAN'S TRUMPET

Miko Imai

CANDLEWICK PRESS

CAMBRIDGE, MASSACHUSETTS

It was the three little bears' birthday. Papa and Mama bear had something special for them.

Theodore
got a drum.

Oswald
got a banjo.

And Sebastian
got a trumpet.

"Let's play
'Happy Birthday!'" they shouted.

Theodore banged on his drum.

Rat-a-tat-tat

Twang

Twang

Oswald strummed his banjo.

And Sebastian
blew into his trumpet.
But the only
sound it
made
was . . .

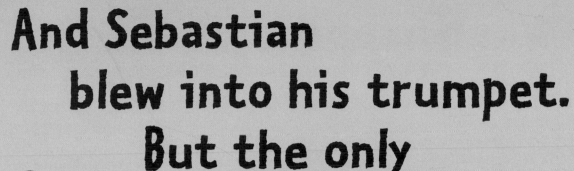

pfffft

Theodore and Oswald
played "Happy Birthday"
for Papa and Mama bear.

Rat-a-tat-tat

Twang

Twang

I wish I could play my trumpet, thought Sebastian.

Pfffffttt

"I HATE this trumpet!" Sebastian sobbed.

"Why did you give me a trumpet,
Mama? It doesn't even work!"

"Maybe you're trying too hard," said Mama bear. "Why don't you rest now and try again later?"

When Sebastian woke up, he couldn't wait to try his trumpet again. He tiptoed toward it.

He picked it up
and started
to play.

TA-
OOOOON!

-TA-TA-
OOOOOOON!

"You did it, Sebastian!"
his brothers shouted.

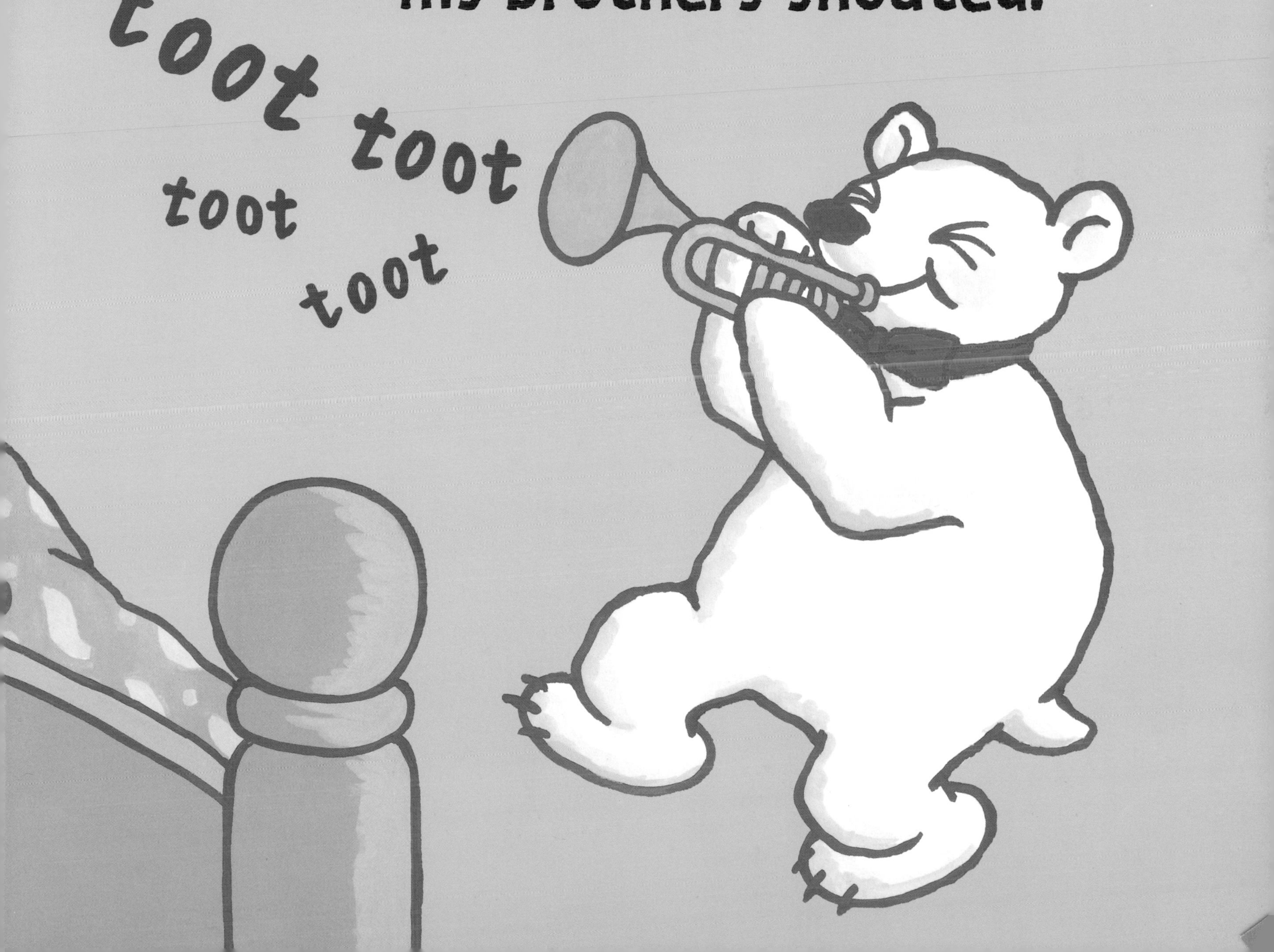

And the three little bears all played "Happy Birthday" together.

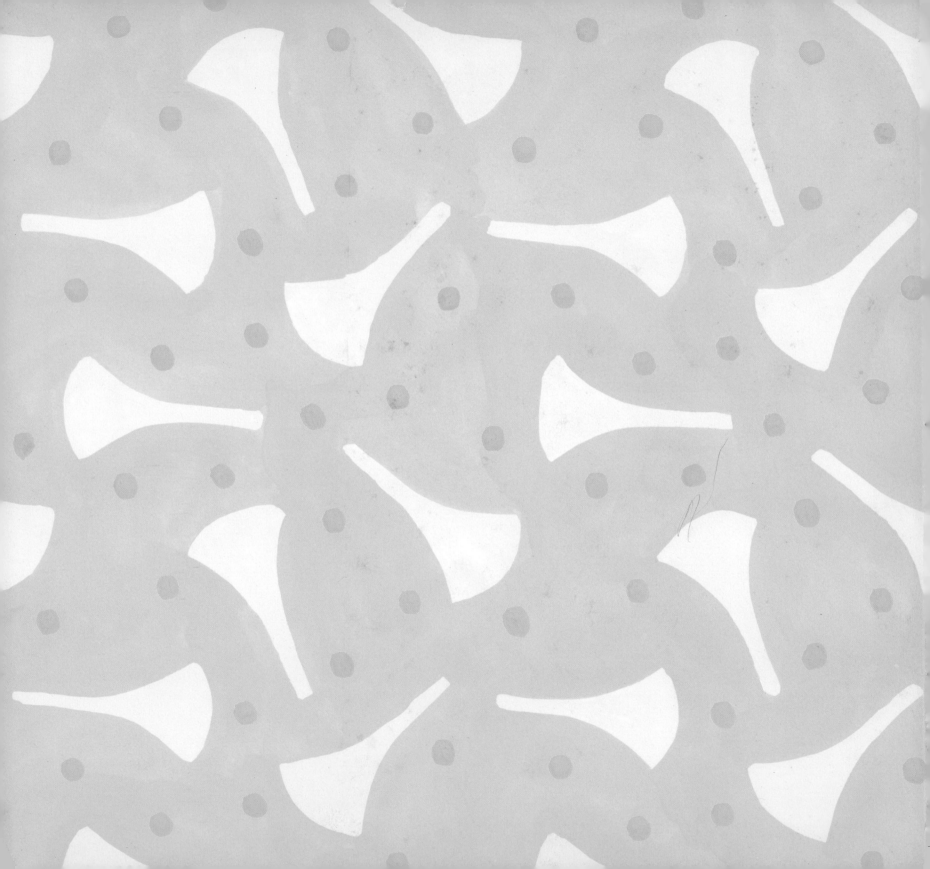